Religious
Death Trap

Peter J. Michael

Religious Death Trap

ISBN-13: 978-0-6459234-4-5

Published by Peter J. Michael

ALL BOOKS BY THIS AUTHOR ARE:

THE GREAT WAR AGAINST TERRORISM

KILLING THE BOGEYMAN I & II

RUTHLESS

RELIGIOUS DEATH TRAP

Religious Death Trap

RELIGIOUS DEATH TRAP

We have yet to deal with our very determined and dangerous foe – that policeman.
And for this cause, we shall initiate the greatest resolve and our deadliest resources in order to deter a waging of war against us, by this enemy of ours named Robert Stewart!
We shall at last see a final solution to our problem: the corpse of Robert Stewart.
And so were the words of Jack Carman, one of several priests who resided in New York City, in Staten Island, under police investigation for crimes relating to cold-and-calculated murder by Commander Robert Stewart.

Jack Carman was a sixty-eight-year-old, medium-built, medium-height grotesque-looking Catholic Priest of American descent, who was accused of murdering a recent American cardinal of the Catholic Church.

Jack Carman was accused of murdering, His Eminence, the Archbishop of New York, having been appointed to that position by the Pope, only six weeks ago.

Jack Carman felt robbed of that position he solely wanted.
And as payback, two weeks ago, he killed the recent Archbishop by poisoning him.

Robert Stewart, investigating corruption within the churches at present, following the police investigation and death of Pastor Blade Blackwood, was also rapidly closing in on the crimes of Priest, Jack Carman.
Robert knew that Jack Carman was jealous of the now dead Archbishop, and was also quite sore at the Pope, who did not choose him (Jack Carman) as newly appointed Archbishop.
But instead, chose someone else.
Thus, Robert Stewart investigated this priest also of committing murder of the foulest variety against the currently dead Archbishop of New York.

Robert Stewart knew the archbishop was poisoned.

It would appear on the surface as though the 70-year-old Archbishop died from a heart attack.

But Robert knew that he was instead poisoned. The poison he was given resulted in him dying from two main left and right coronary arteries supplying blood to his heart becoming fatally blocked.

The very thorough autopsy examinations still underway, were bound to prove that.

Poison was always a very popular method of killing one's enemies.

One of them, anyhow.

Poisons can be administered in large doses or small doses.

In drinks, in food, in ventilation systems via poisonous gas fumes and so forth.

Robert Stewart knew (despite Jack Carman's assumptions), no poison could or would remain undetected by the exorbitant testing he insisted be carried out upon the dead body.

The New York City Office of Chief Medical Examiner was brought in on the case to conduct independent investigations using advanced forensic science unto the dead Archbishop's corpse, until the thorough autopsy identified not only what poison he was given, but to also nail Jack Carman as

responsible for administering that poison to the dead Cardinal, Archbishop of New York.
And to in fact nail Jack Carman for murder.
Robert wanted to know which poison Jack Carman used to kill the Archbishop of New York, and make his death instead resemble a heart attack.
Was it Arsenic?
Was it Cyanide?
Was it Oleander?
Was it Ethylene Glycol?
Was it Thallium?
Or was it Polonium-210?

Robert was determined to discover the truth and nail Jack Carman to the wall for murder!

And Catholic Priest Jack Carman was equally determined to ensure that Commander Robert Stewart did not find out the truth and discover the real damning evidence linking him to the crime!

So, Jack Carman was brainstorming some drastic measures in order to not only save himself from a lifetime in prison or worse - the death penalty - but to also eliminate that one threat against him: Commander Robert Stewart!

And Jack Carman was discussing his secret murderous plans inside his church in Staten Island, with four other priests whom aided and abetted Jack Carman with equal complicity to the Late Archbishop's demise.

Jack Carman insisted to his aiders: First, let us remember those who will never come back to us.
Let us remember the precious life of Pastor Blade Blackwood.
And his brother Thorn Blackwood.
And all those who contributed to our wealth via hefty donations to our churches.
Let us never forget the value of their lives to us.
And let us never forget the man who took such people away from us.
That cop.
Robert Stewart!
And now he seeks to destroy us as well.
We cannot sit back and let this happen.
We must show courage and unity in our cause to rid ourselves of this menacing cop.
Even if it means we need to sacrifice our lives in order to accomplish this most important death of that pest, now threatening our livelihoods and our very existences, then sacrificing our lives - WE WILL DO!

Robert Stewart is a merciless enemy.
We must show endurance against him.
We must not lose faith in Almighty God's
assistance to us in killing Robert Stewart.
God will help us help ourselves to murder this
dire fellow to our cause and causes.
Let us remember our benefactors and the
services they provided to us.
Let us remember how Robert Stewart took
those friends away from us.
Through prison.
Through death – by his weapons of war against
us and his all-evil Justice System!
And through his cold-hearted brutality he has
demonstrated against our precious old friends.
And the callous monstrosity he now targets us
with.
We have come to the end of our tribulation.
I say that we must kill our foe and kill ourselves
in the process.
We must form a holy suicide pact to save
ourselves.

May God grant us the strength to carry our
plans successfully in saving ourselves through a
rapid death – and to also save this world by
killing that cop who is a threat to everyone who
resides in it!

God Almighty help us!
God Almighty – deliver us to Paradise upon
our deaths.
And please deliver Robert Stewart to the Lake
of Fire for forcing our hands in committing
suicide in order to save ourselves from his evil
Justice System!
Save us, O God.
And kill our enemy Robert Stewart!
Strike him hard with your weapons of war!
Break his teeth.
Smash his bones!
Mentally retard his brain so he can no longer
concoct ways to harm us priests!
Tear his arms and his legs off his body so he
can no longer fight us.
O Dear God – deliver us from that bad man's
wrath against us.
Save us from the cunning mastery of that evil
cop's intentions against us.
And please O merciful God, save us from the
vengeance directed our way by all bad police
officers.
We are priests.
We are good people.
And those bad policemen want to harm us.
They want to destroy us.
Please Almighty One, do not forsake us in our
time of need.

Cripple the hands and feet of our police foes so they cannot destroy us.
Castrate all our enemies and dismember their bodies from head to foot.
Please forsake us not.
And do not allow those police who want to persecute us go on living any longer.
Do not let them go unpunished!

Now my fellow priestly brothers - let us prepare for the death that is to come.
Let us ready ourselves for the deaths that await us.
We must all be devoted to this common purpose.
And I have come prepared.
Fear not my priestly companions.
We are not here unarmed and helpless.
But we are gathered here today armed with a powerful bomb.
My good friend the Late Thorn Blackwood had kept me well armed in a time of need.
He supplied me with our weapons of war when we needed them.
And the bomb has a timer attached to it.
The countdown has begun.
The bomb is seated beneath one of the wooden chairs inside this church.

And Robert Stewart is tied helpless inside the confessional.
I was waiting for him last night outside his home.
When he finished his day's work at the police station, spending the day trying to obtain evidence against us, I snuck outside his home.
I was hidden on the other side of the road behind a tree.
When he arrived at night and parked his car in the driveway of his home, I was waiting for him.
As soon as he stepped out of his car, I pointed my GLOCK 17 pistol firearm toward his back and fired six shots.
The gun had a silencer, also known as a sound suppressor, so no one could hear me shoot him down.
Then I took the body with me inside the boot of my car.
I carried the profusely bleeding body inside this church.
I hid him inside the confessional.

It is Tuesday.
The church is quiet.
No interference from anyone.
I let him bleed for hours inside the confessional.

He is unconscious.
He cannot move.
If he is not already dead from all that blood pouring out of his body, he will be dead soon once that bomb detonates to explode this entire church building to pieces - taking our lives and the life of that cop with it!
No one saw me take his body.
No one knows we are here.
We are safe.
We will die shortly.
That cop will die too!
We will surely remain devoted to our common purpose of this suicide pact between us.
We have fought, struggled - but endured our hardships successfully to our utmost capabilities.

Once we blow up this church taking the life of that cop away from threatening this world any further - every man, woman and civilian child who remains on this earth will be forever grateful to us.
No one will ever have to contend with the nemesis of that damning cop any longer.
He will never arrest any of us ever again.
He will never kill any of us ever again!

We must carry out our duties of killing and
being killed, unflinchingly.

We will do this world a great deed.
Because much is at stake right now.
Robert Stewart has caused many criminals
much suffering and peril by his perverted
crusade against us all.
Certainly, he put us all in great jeopardy: our
freedoms.
Our independence.
Our very existences in a Free Society.
To live our lives as we choose: as free people.
He robbed us all of our free will.
Now, we will rob him of his evil tenacity to
destroy us too, as he did to our sacred brothers
and sisters before us.
Certainly, this generation and generations after
us will remember this day.
They will be forever grateful to us!

And be thankful in the knowledge that just as
this day we have vowed to defend ourselves, we
have also taken it upon ourselves to defend the
liberties of everyone in this Great State of ours,
who would constantly be made target by this
greatest of burdens to those brothers and
sisters of our universe.

By ridding this country-this world of that one burdensome cop, we will be looked upon as heroes for many generations to come.

Our cause is a cause for everyone where freedom is cherished.

And freedom of speech, freedom of action and freedom of law and liberty of our friendly neighbours go hand in hand.

We will no longer be enslaved by rules and regulations that go against our interests.
We will no longer be burdened by crazy suffocating laws which confine us and ruin our freedoms.
We must have faith in a better world after we depart from this harsh existence.
Once we reach the afterlife, we will no longer be enslaved, abandoned and isolated by the evil laws upheld by that one evil crusading cop, who has cast so many of our people before us into oblivion.

We must have confidence in our faith in Almighty God's mercy delivered towards us.

We must trust that he has prepared a better life for us in the hereafter.

And we must trust that he has a sufficient punishment installed against that one evil policeman who has pushed our backs against the wall, by forcing us to end our lives as we will do shortly.

Robert Stewart has caused our world and its people much suffering by the tyranny of the unjust laws he has upheld against us.

But, in the end, we will not falter in our final necessary decisions to be made, without fail.

So, let us keep faith and unity, not only with ourselves, but with Almighty God, who will strengthen our resolve in carrying out our joined suicide pact we have this day formed between us much successfully.
And to deliver us to victory!

And with the death of Robert Stewart, we will finally restore peace and sanity into this world and the freedoms of thought and actions by our people, currently burdened by this very saddened earth!

And the ordeals that the people of our laws have endured by this man, will be endured no more, from this day forward!

And with resolve, willpower and inexhaustive vitality to our beliefs, we must carry out our deaths gladly.
For this day, we will be united forever in Paradise with the God of our fathers, who will bestow us with a great reward for our suffering and sacrifice to be made right now.
That one Reward awaiting us, brings me great comfort!
Our hour of danger will soon pass.
Thank you, God! – for both your understanding and your mercy!

Catholic Priest Jack Carman from Staten Island, New York believed that his war against Robert Stewart could only end with the defeat of Robert Stewart.
He vowed to remove Robert's complete strength in the capacity to ever act aggressively against him and his people again - **forever!**
It would be a total defeat of his foe!

Jack Carman considered Robert Stewart a dark peril subjected to the world.
He considered Robert was the bad guy and that he (the Catholic Priest) was doing the world a service by killing him.

Jack Carman planned to change the rules of the game of Robert's war.

Whereby, just as Robert was always on the offensive against him and his world's people and their laws, the Catholic Priest intended to have Robert retreat from any further assaults driven towards them, by killing him!

'All depends on me!' – were the words of Jack Carman.

As all others before me failed, I shall succeed in the mighty task of killing that man.
I will destroy him!
I will annihilate him!
I will finally rid this earth from the likes of his deadly clutches!

Jack Carman had shot Robert Stewart six times outside his home, then kidnapped his profusely bleeding body and dumped him inside the confessional of his church in Staten Island.

The Catholic Priest planned to kill himself with four other priests in a joined suicide pact, taking Robert's life with them, by a very powerful planted bomb inside the church, set to go off shortly via a twenty-four-hour timer system countdown connected to it.

'You Robert Stewart have caused suffering to my brothers and sisters for the last time!' - cursed Jack Carman.

You will not defeat us in the end.
But this time, you will be the one to face complete defeat by my hands.

I want complete annihilation!
I want that policeman to be exterminated quickly with no fuss!
I want Robert Stewart obliterated from this earth at once!
I will shake the foundations of his existence!
He deserves to pass away!

You think you will succeed in putting me in prison like you did with all the others?
You think you will kill me as you killed so many of our fellow men before us?
No.
No, Robert Stewart.
This war you have now declared against the Church will not come to an end the way you imagine, via the destruction of us priests.

But it will come only with the end of us all.
Because you will not kill us.
We will kill ourselves.
And we will take your dead body with us.
Yes.

We will die, not your way, but our way!
And you will die with us.

At exactly the same time we go, you go out of
this world too!

This time you will be exterminated, policeman!
You will be annihilated with one very powerful
bomb!
Unlike the others, I do not concede to luck.
I form my own luck.
You have destroyed so many of our brothers
and sisters before us.
You hear my words?

Unlike other priests, I do not label my fellow
supporters as, my son!
Or…
My daughter!
No.
I refer to them as brothers and sisters.
I treat people equally.

I consider them all of equal rank and status, regardless of their pasts and backgrounds and standing in life.

I forgive everyone for everything.
That is me.

I bless them all!

And these are the people you have targeted to destruction, policeman.
You destroyed very powerful people throughout your horrible days as an officer of the law.

You destroyed Mafia bosses.
You destroyed gangsters.
You destroyed powerful politicians.
You destroyed my friends: The Blackwood family.

Remember Pastor Blade Blackwood and his brother Thorn Blackwood.
They were my friends.
And they too became casualties by your destructive hands.

All dead because of you!

But unlike the others, I will not let myself be
destroyed by you.
No, policeman!
This time I dictate the terms.

And as everyone else had failed, I will succeed
in terminating your life from this world, once
and for all!

And with iron will, unflinching determination
and great focus, I will be the one to attack you,
before you attack me.
That is the task at hand for me.
And yes, I am succeeding.
I am a representative of the church.
That means, that I have God on my side.
That is why I have succeeded in destroying you,
when all others have only failed.
Your death is inevitable, policeman!
Hell awaits you, for your life of crime in
attempting to condemn me as you have so
many of my brothers and sisters before me!

You have arrested and killed so many of my
friends in the past;
People who donated to the church and kept the
parish what it is today: a thriving entity.
You destroyed them all, our greatest supporters
and sponsors.

And now you seek to attack the Church.
You have a lot of nerve to do this.
It is not enough you have destroyed so many
benefactors of the church.

Now you seek to declare war against the
Church itself.

You call us priests criminals.
You say we are corrupt!

But that is not true, policeman!

We are not criminals.
We are servants of God.

You, policeman - YOU – are the criminal!
I will punish you.

You underestimated me terribly.
You underestimated the power of the oldest
institution of the world: meaning the sacred
church and its followers.

You think you can declare war against the
Church and its priests and get away with it?
No.
Not this time, policeman!

You think you will expose us priests as criminals and destroy us economically?
You want us to lose our jobs and be thrown into the streets as beggars before you then plunge us like rag dolls into your prison cell!
You think you will defeat the all-powerful Church?
Do you seriously believe I will allow you to inflict upon us priests the same catastrophic defeats you caused to so many powerful people throughout this country in the past?
That will not happen.
You will not destroy the sanctimonious priesthood – and drive us priests to unemployment.

Many of us priests are unskilled to obtain any other profession.
You will not bring the church to economic ruin by your current attacks against it and us priests.

The burden you attempt to impose against us by labelling us as 'corrupt' will come to a standstill when I end your life.

You will not close the doors of our churches.
You will not stop the donations driven to us by our brothers and sisters throughout the general community.

You will not drive us priests to poverty, misery, starvation and homelessness by your current attacks against us.

We will remain a powerful institution against your tyranny recently directed towards us, policeman!

Like many people in this country, I came from a poor family background.
I was homeless.
I was a starving child before I decided to join the church and make real money to feed my belly.
I built a very large cliental who see me regularly.
The public trusts me.
They tell me all their secrets.
They need fear nothing from me.
I do not judge!
I only counsel and forgive them all for anything and everything they have done in the past and continue doing.
I bless them all.
And in return, they open up their wallets to me.
I don't care if they kill, steal, rape and sell drugs to children.
I do not care for the police.
I keep their secrets.
I forgive them all.

These people are my congregation.
My fellow man.
And woman.
I bless them all.
In return, the public who deal with me share a mutual trust with me.
They open their hearts and donate a lot of money to me.
And you threatened to take that all away from me, policeman!
You planned to destroy it all.
You conspired to destroy me and my fellow priest colleagues – just as you destroyed Pastor Blade Blackwood – who was a very dear trusted friend of mine.
Now he is dead.
And for that and your attempts to also claim my life from me much the same way, I will kill you, policeman!
The church was my refuge.
It was always my safe haven.

You will not enter these walls of this sacred House of God and defile it with your police badge and your police gun and bullets.
This is Holy Ground.
I will stab you in the eyes with my heavy real gold crucifix, you little devil.

I will end your evil crusade by throwing Holy Water on your face and stabbing you with a stake through your very black heart.

The Catholic Church was around for a very long time – for approximately two thousand years.
It has been in power for many, many centuries.
It is the one powerful institution of the world that has remained untouched forever.
You - you irritating policeman - seriously think you will kick down the doors of these sacred walls and cause this powerhouse to come crumbling down?
That will never happen, you little policeman!
The misery you wish to bestow upon the Church is appalling.
You left me no choice, but to end your life, you extremely irritating policeman.

My fellow priestly friends - just give me a small number of hours before passing judgement against me.

Because before the next evening is through, I will solve all your problems by eliminating this one diabolical threat to your lives.

And may Almighty God look mercifully upon
our actions and our deeds.

Redeem us from this demon before us and lead
the rest of your servants of the Church to
eternal peace - upon our deaths - which will
unfold in just a matter of hours now.

Almighty God;
The excitement I feel in my heart to leaving this
world and reuniting with you in Heaven brings
me more joy and happiness than you can
possibly ever truly imagine.

I am so happy to face death very shortly.

The prospect of meeting God in the hereafter
fills my heart with such gladness.

O, how I so wish to embrace the Lord of my
fathers when I see him in the eternal home of
The Kingdom of God!

First, my priestly friends and I will suffer on
earth for our God.
Then, we will enter the eternal home to spend
forever in nirvana with our one true Master!

Me and my colleagues worship you as our final
Salvation and Saviour.

My God;
Look down on our trials and tribulations.
Forsake us not in our hour of pain and grief.
What we do on earth at this moment, is not
only out of hatred for those wicked men and
women on earth who wish to attack us.
But what we do is mostly out of selfless love
for our Church and our God!
So, please God, listen to the pleas of your
priests.
Watch our torments.
And bring us strength out of the darkness, so
that in only a matter of hours now we may
enter your kingdom to finally see the LIGHT!

O, my Lord;
I will spend the last-remaining hours of my life
praying to thee.
You will deliver us from the burdens of
bondage by this dreadful police officer who has
harassed us priests inside our House of
Worship.
Amen!

But before I die, it is my solemn task to make
sure that this miserable, black-hearted

policeman and all his evil police colleagues'
attempts at dismantling our church, be rectified
through the death and destruction of this
lawman I have brought here to face death – as
an example of what will happen should anyone
ever again attempt to attack the Church in the
future!

I will not allow this petty policeman to result in
the disintegration of our Holy Church!
And I will see to it that all his search and arrest
warrants directed at the Church are torn in half.

The lunacy, insanity, misery and dreadfulness of
the state's police forces will become impotent
against us!

And once I die before long, taking that
catastrophic police officer's life with me, the
Church will become solidified to grow much
stronger and more powerful than ever before –
for thousands more years to come.

Fear not, my priestly comrades!
I will stamp out all judicial opposition from the
Church.
The police will not investigate the Church any
longer.

But the Church will mock and steamroll all
local police forces.
The Church must control all such powers that
otherwise work to threaten its existence.

You police cannot see me.
You cannot see what has become of your
fellow police commander I have hidden within
these church walls to die with me shortly.
But I can see you police.
I feel your panic-stricken minds.
I know you will soon discover this policeman's
disappearance and conduct an active search
party across the entire state to hunt for his
whereabouts.

But before you can find him, it will be too late.
That bomb planted here within these church
walls will detonate exploding the church, us
priests inside – and also claiming the life of that
menacing esteemed colleague of yours.
That death will shock you all!
It will surprise you very deeply.
It will distress your minds, your hearts and your
souls.
But you must always remember **that death** as a
token of future warnings against you all.

**DO NOT EVER MAKE THE MISTAKE
TO ATTEMPT TO ATTACK THE
CHURCH AGAIN IN THE FUTURE, OR
YOU WILL ALL END UP THE SAME
WAY AS AN EXAMPLE TO THE TOTAL
SUM OF YOU, THAT WE WILL NOT
BE TOYED WITH!**

Upon the death of this policeman here, the
Church's notoriety will become re-established
as the supreme Global Power of the world.
And you police and your courts of law will
become reduced to second-class citizens and
second-class powers.

The world will become educated in laws of
'favouritism' and 'prejudice'.
They will look up to the churches of all
cultures.
And, they will look down on all other so-called
powers such as the police and the government.

Any future opposition to the Church and its
leaders will become brutally and ruthlessly
crushed and eliminated!
We will defeat and imprison you policemen.
Not the other way around.

Anyone who ever dares to attack the Church in the future with threatening actions, even menacing words, calling it a house of liars and devil worshippers ever again will be killed.

Anyone who tries to criticise and investigate the Church must be seen as threats to God's Word.
They must be eliminated at once.
And their deaths must be made to be seen as ordained by the orders of God himself!

The police and its legislative bodies within the local, state and federal governments are all communists.
We will outsmart them.
We will smash them all!

'I believe it was God's will that allowed this policeman to attack me, so that I can have him killed – and therefore as a result, safeguard the power of the Church, by using that one death as an example to others, to never attempt to bring down the Church to its knees ever again in the future!' – cursed Jack Carman.

Killing this policeman at the same time as I will take my life for my Lord and God, is truly the proudest day of my life.

This horrible policeman has mentioned my name to all his fellow police comrades. Therefore, it is imperative that I not only kill this threatening foe of mine, but I must also kill myself before his colleagues figure out the truth and then look to kill me.
I will die my may, NOT THEIRS!

You will not call us corrupt priests any longer. The Church will strip away your hatred for us any way possible!
You police are so foolish!
You will no longer oppress us with your communistic ways and brutal fascism!
I demand that it must cease!
No longer will there be restraint on our part!
We will be worshipped by young and old alike!
We will be looked upon as the creators of the world – as saviours and noble men of the most powerful institution in the world, called the Catholic Church!

In the meantime, we are left with no alternative but to attack and kill this little policeman – at the same time we must kill ourselves inside this church - in a united suicide pact that is formed between us brotherly priests!

And after we die, taking the life of this wretched police official with us, every other prospective enemy in the future will grow weak and cowardly to ever face the Church in opposition again.

All enemies of the Church's priests are little worms.

They are parasites and leeches.

As I have extended mercy and pity to those members of the public who confess their sins to me – at the same time I will display utter contempt and brutal ruthlessness to those who oppose me.

I will attack them with much greater intensity than their attacks directed my way.

Meaning this little policeman here!

His life will end in total ruin, absolute destruction and complete obliteration!

I am right.

And the police and government who oppose me are wrong.

They will lose a life of theirs.

And via my death to be orchestrated shortly, I will achieve a complete **VICTORY!**

'I DECLARE WAR AGAINST YOU POLICE!' – SHOUTED JACK CARMAN MUCH JUBILANTLY.

Leave us alone and surrender, or you will be destroyed alongside this pest of a dying policeman I have locked up within the walls of this church.

Anyone who opposes us will be snatched up with the same method of surprise that I snatched this policeman, just hours before! And that will become a historic lesson of mastery for you all as payment for your wickedness directed against us!
We are the formidable enemy, not the other way around.

Now, the time of death has arrived!

Jack Carman and his four Catholic Priest partners in crime, remained inside the church for the duration of the twenty-four-hour ticking time bomb planted inside the premises.
They did not leave to even purchase any food or drink the entire time.
And in the final hour, that evening before midnight, when the countdown was due to finish, BUT NOW, only moments prior the bomb detonation being scheduled, Jack Carman and the four Catholic Priests, dressed in their black-coloured priestly garments,

situated with him, huddled around the blood-soaked unconscious body of Robert Stewart inside the confessional.
They glanced at the motionless being of their foe and looked at themselves smiling.

They embraced each other one last time and then the bomb planted inside detonated the entire church, taking their lives together with Robert's Stewart's body, in one gigantic fireball of explosive boiling flames, mixed with grey-and-black coloured ash, that shook the entire city of New York much like an erupting volcano.

Its mighty powerful impact of a blast and consecutive blasts for moments thereafter, frightened all the local residents out of their comfort zones, and many from their beds who were asleep, all suddenly forced to life in sheer panic – until the source of that terrifying big bang was confirmed by the police and local news reporters, to be the source of the Catholic Church inside Staten Island bursting in flames and being smashed to pieces by one big powerful bomb, claiming the lives of five priests who were situated inside at the time, together with the precious life of one of their heroes called: Robert Stewart!

No one knew how the bomb was planted or detonated until a police investigation into the shocking incident concluded the accurate findings of a suicide pact by five priests, together taking the life of the one crusading cop who was investigating them for committing heinous crimes within the Church.

When it was confirmed that Robert Stewart was dead, it sent disheartening shock waves throughout the entire country.
No one was hit harder emotionally than all the members of the police precinct he served – and especially his beloved family back home in Brooklyn who reeled over the news in utter mourning, disbelief and much dread at the utterly surprising and shocking news that their beloved Robert Stewart was extinct, nonliving and perished.

The horrible news struck them all in the core of their beings with the same intensity matching the very strong bomb blast Robert was reported to have been killed by.
It shook their minds and hearts with the same powerful and destructive impact.
It was just pure disbelief.

The suddenness of it, together mixed with the surprise of such an event was still unable to be comprehended by many for some time to come.
They grieved the loss in what seemed unending powerful emotions of profuse misery.

Only one more unfavourable outcome was drawn in all this: sometimes in this world in which they lived, considering the sort of horrible human beings which surrounded them from all walks of life – that mere concept of **'life'** just did not always carry with it a happy ending!

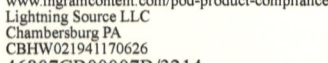